Who has been whipping frail Sasha Ivan? James Budd and Honey Mack are determined to find out. They discover the truth about Sasha's cruel Aunt Ada, but is it the whole truth? A mysterious gypsy, a runaway tractor, a knife expertly aimed at James's head, and Sasha's regal looks and behavior all lead James to suspect something more. Only by traveling to the exotic land of Mornia can James, Honey, and Sasha track down the answer to THE MYSTERY OF THE LOST PRINCESS.

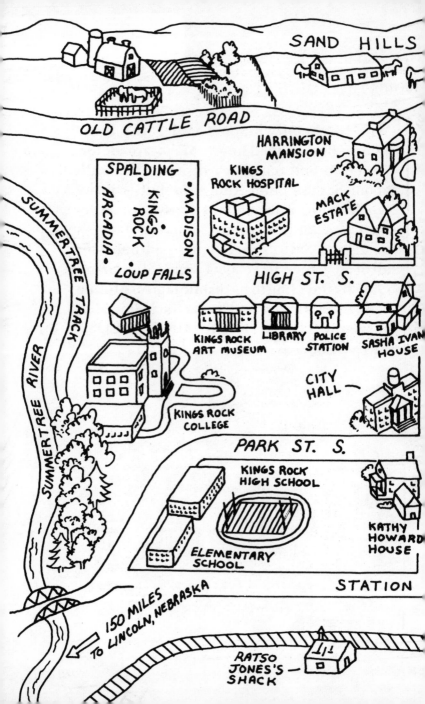

KINGS ROCK

ROCK
BLUFFS

KAWABATA FARM

OLD CATTLE ROAD

ALLEYWAY

THE
STAR AGENCY
(JAMES)

ALDA
HOUSE

KINGS ROCK TIMES

THE HUT

MISS TONI'S FASHIONS

TORELLO'S HARDWARE

ORPHEUM MOVIE THEATER

HIGH STREET

HIGH ST. N.

THE
GREEN

CHURCH

BANDSTAND

W

S   N

LION PRIDE STATUE

E

NORTH LOUP RIVER

PARK   ST.

PARK ST. N.

DRUGS

PELL'S

STARLIGHT THEATER

MADISON BANK

HARDING DRUG STORE

PELL'S DEPT. STORE

FAST FOOD

ARCADE

SHOPPING PLAZA

ROAD

LODEN AIRPORT

JAMES BUDD

3

THE MYSTERY OF
THE LOST
PRINCESS

THE MYSTERY OF
THE LOST
PRINCESS

By Dale Carlson

**Illustrated by
Tom LaPadula**

**Cover illustration by
Chuck Liese**

A GOLDEN BOOK • NEW YORK
**WESTERN PUBLISHING COMPANY, INC.,
RACINE, WISCONSIN 53404**

For Doris Duenewald
a princess herself
with love and gratitude always

Contents

THE MYSTERY OF
THE LOST
PRINCESS

CHAPTER ONE

A Child Is Hurt

There were angry red welts again on Sasha's pale, thin back. The abuse was so fresh, and Sasha's thinness so startling, that Honey didn't know whether it was easier to count the welts or Sasha's ribs.

This time I'm going to tell James, Honey promised Sasha Ivan silently. *James Budd will know what to do. James always does.*

"Sasha?" Honey said, this time aloud.

Sasha jumped at Honey's voice, as though she were afraid of any human sound. She quickly pulled her gray sweater over the thin arms and shoulders, down over the gray skirt. Her gym locker was right next to Honey's, and Honey felt Sasha would have fled at the first mention of her name, only she wasn't quite finished dressing.

"Sasha!"

17

But Honey Mack's voice only echoed along the empty row of lockers. The sweet, haunted-looking girl with her soft, raven-black hair and smoky green eyes had given Honey a strange half-smile — and then she was gone.

James Budd was waiting for Honey on the front steps of the gym, on the most gorgeous day the wide skies over Nebraska had yet produced. Honey thought there was a tie between James and the day. In her opinion — and in the opinion of most of the females she had polled — James Budd was the handsomest creation Nebraska had produced.

He was clean-cut, with a strong jaw, wide, dark eyes, and black hair. James was not violent by nature, but he was a stubborn fighter for what he felt was right. He knew basic judo and karate, the arts of unarmed self-defense, in case of necessity. He bore a two-inch scar on his tanned forehead from an old fight. He was not only good-looking, Honey reflected, he was also an all-round athlete and a straight-A student, and he dressed well.

"Don't think I don't know what you mean when you look at me like that," said James. He put an arm around Honey's slender waist, trailing his fingers through the waist-length honey-gold hair that gave Honey her name. Honey Mack, too, was more than the prettiest girl in Kings Rock High School's junior class. She was also the fastest runner, the fastest — and best — driver, a writer for the *Kings Rock Times*, and, best of all, James was once in a while heard to say, "She's my girl."

"You're pretty terrific, too," he said now. Then, seeing her expression change from admiring to troubled, he asked, "What is it?"

"Sasha Ivan," Honey replied. "She gave me the oddest smile just now — and then she ran. I wonder if the smile was to thank me for caring, or to ask for help."

She described to James the way Sasha's back looked, the raised, angry stripes from shoulder to waist. "And it wasn't the first time I've seen those welts," Honey added. "But the ones today were the worst."

"What do you know about her?" James asked. "Her friends, her life?"

"I don't think she has any of either," Honey answered. "As far as I know, Sasha comes to school and goes right home to that dreadful Mrs. Ivan in that depressing house."

"Well," said James, his protective feelings

roused by Honey's description of their class-mate's pain, "we'll just go check in at the office after school. Then we'll pay Sasha and Mrs. Ivan a visit."

The office James was referring to was the Star Agency. James Budd, at sixteen, was not only the adopted son of the famous private detective Sam Star, but his right-hand man. After school, during vacations, and when-ever Sam was away on a case, James worked for or took over for Sam. People in Kings Rock, all over Nebraska and the Midwest, and — since their last case, *The Secret of Operation Brain* — in parts of Europe were as used to seeing James Budd on a case as Sam Star.

"James is a born fixer," Sam always said. "He can't leave well enough, or anything else, alone. And if there's no trouble to fix," he would add, "leave it to James, he'll make some."

Honey worked with James and for Sam, too, writing up their cases, often for publica-tion in the *Kings Rock Times*.

As the two climbed into James Budd's red 1971 Pontiac Firebird after school, Honey glanced at James with a worried frown.

"Mrs. Ivan is some kind of religious fanatic," said Honey. "I once took a dare and ran up to one of her windows when I was little. It was really awful inside, dark, with a lot of crucifixions and altars and candles. Did you know Mrs. Ivan adopted Sasha when she was little?"

"Well, then, it means Sasha was born independent like I was," said James. "All that means is you get to turn out as terrific as you like. We'll just have to show her how."

James's teasing remark about being born independent was the only way he ever spoke of being orphaned by parents he never knew. At the age of four, he had been adopted out of an orphanage by Sam Star.

Sam, Honey, and Charlie Alda, the electronics genius of their class and James's best friend, were James's family now. The only other family member was the Firebird, almost totally rebuilt by Charlie, and James's most beloved possession.

They were a noticeable threesome in Kings Rock: the red Firebird, Honey Mack, and James Budd. Tall, slim, and elegant in their matching white running clothes, James and Honey were a visible twosome now as they drove from school on Park Street South, past the Green, and up High Street, to the Star Agency.

They ran up the front porch steps and into the front hall. To the left of the front hall was Sam and James's large leather-and-brass living room. To the right were the Star Agency's offices. The bedrooms were upstairs, the kitchen and Sam's rose garden in the back. James went through the waiting room into the back consultation office to see Sam. Honey picked up the mail in the front office with a quick swoop and went to join them.

"Not here," said James. "Just this."

It was a note from Sam. It read: *Been called in on a Missing Princess case. Have flown Frankovna, capital of Mornia, principality in eastern Europe, for details. Mind the store. Love to Honey. Sam.*

With the note was Sam's hand-drawn map. It was rough, but exact. Mornia was a tiny postage stamp of a kingdom, obviously overlooked when the larger territorial boundaries were set, nestled in a corner between Hungary, Czechoslovakia, and Russia.

Also with the note was a small photograph

of a dark-haired little girl with big, sad eyes.

"What is he up to now?" James sighed.

He adored Sam. He could just picture the small, wiry, sharp-eyed man pushing back his ever-present gray felt fedora as he wrote the note. Sam didn't hit. He didn't use guns. He was the smartest man James had ever met. And his opinion was the only one on earth James cared about besides his own.

"James?" said Honey, pleading gently.

"Sure, come on," said James.

They drove south on High Street, past the Green. The Ivan house was right at the corner of High Street South and Southbend Avenue. It stood at the bottom of the Hill, the part of Southbend Avenue where the rich and prominent Kings Rock families like the Harringtons and the Macks — Honey's family — had their estates.

The Ivan house wasn't one of these estates, nor was it one of Kings Rock's ordinary homes. Set far back on a large lot vaulted over with old elms, climbing bittersweet vines, and roses, it looked like something out of the dark end of a fairy tale.

James and Honey crept through the

hedges toward the old house. Before they reached the front door, however, James heard a sound.

He held his finger to his mouth and shook his head, signaling Honey not to speak.

There was the sound again.

It was a low, drawn-out moan — the sound of pain.

CHAPTER TWO

James Has an Idea

The moan came from the potting shed at the back of the garden. James made for it swiftly. In his white running clothes, James looked like a knight in shining armor, Honey thought, loving James for his quickness to protect the undefended.

"Undefended is right," she muttered grimly when she and James saw what was in the shed.

"I'm going to break the window. Move back," said James, his voice low with rage.

He cracked the window easily with a rock, then brushed away enough glass to reach inside. He turned the lock and let himself and Honey into the small, dark shed.

It was full of clay pots, flats, bags of soil and vermiculite, fertilizer, hoses, and other equipment to nurture the soil. It also contained a chair with leather straps, equipment not to nurture but to punish a child. James, who generally kept his feelings under control, was nauseated with horror.

"Who did this? Who tied you up in here, Sasha?" he asked.

As he spoke, he quickly undid the tight leather straps from Sasha's wrists and feet. Though the straps had cut through her thin flesh, Sasha made no outcry.

She gave no answer, either.

"Won't you tell us, Sasha?" Honey asked gently. She brushed Sasha's damp hair back from her forehead and pulled the girl close to her for comfort.

Sasha cried silently, but only for a moment or two. Then she straightened up, gathered herself together, and to James and Honey's astonishment, behaved as if two friends had simply, if unexpectedly, come to call.

"Won't you come into the house?" she said cordially. "Do let me offer you tea. Perhaps you'll meet Aunt Ada. I call her my aunt, you know, because Mrs. Ivan was kind enough to adopt me."

Gracious as a lady fresh from her drawing room, rather than a child who'd just been

imprisoned in a potting shed, Sasha led James and Honey into the Victorian front parlor.

James looked around at the dimly lit room, cluttered with stiff chairs, hard little sofas, tables full of old photographs and bric-a-brac. There was barely room for people. Heavy drapes held out the sunlight, and the feeble fire held off none of the cold.

"Bloody depressing," James said under his breath to Honey.

But if the room had been dreary at first entrance, the appearance of a tall, gaunt woman in a high-collared, long, black dress made it worse.

"Aunt Ada, I'd like you to meet my friends James Budd and Honey Mack. They're in my class at school. James, Honey, I'd like you to meet my aunt, Mrs. Ivan," said Sasha.

James was startled at Sasha's easy formality. They'd all been taught proper introductions, but, James realized, they almost never used them. Sasha, however, sounded as if she'd been *born* murmuring socially correct phrases. It was especially bizarre, James thought, considering that Sasha must be in terrible pain.

"You'd never guess what she's just been through," Honey murmured to James, as she walked across the room with her hand held out to Mrs. Ivan. Aloud, she said, "How do you do, Mrs. Ivan. I'm delighted to meet you."

James, too, swung forward and acknowledged the introduction.

During the formalities of introductions and Mrs. Ivan's offer of tea, James watched keenly every flicker of expression on his hostess's face. What made James so valuable to Sam as a detective was that he noticed and mentally recorded things that most people missed.

What James saw now was an entire silent conversation between Sasha and her adoptive aunt.

Did you tell? was the question.

Not a word, was the answer.

Are you sure? came the threatening return stare.

I'm sure, came the frightened return answer.

When Mrs. Ivan swept from the room, as severe and forbidding as the house she lived in, Honey took a look at the walls of the room and shuddered. All those paintings of flagellations, whippings, martyrdoms, and crucifixions! All those pictures of pain made her flesh crawl with fear. James looked, too, then turned his attention back to Sasha.

When her aunt left the room, Sasha for a single moment finally showed the pain, fear, and immense tiredness she felt. She slumped into a chair, then quickly righted herself, once more gracious and smiling.

But James saw that moment and spoke.

"Sasha, does your aunt beat you? Honey told me about the marks on your back, so there's no need to lie. Let us help you. You don't have to live like this," he said gently. "We'll help you. There are laws, things that can be done to protect you."

Sasha's expression didn't change.

"No, it isn't my aunt who beats me. She's the one trying to protect me. She's always taken care of me, and she says she always will. I trust her, truly I do, James. But thank you both very much for caring," said Sasha. "Of course, she's as angry about the beatings as you are, and she'll be furious when I tell her about the shed again. Only this problem is a family secret. James, Honey, please don't pry. It can do no good."

The slight accent, the gentleness of Sasha's tone, almost hid the fear and hopelessness in her eyes. "You see," she added in a whisper, looking around to make certain she wouldn't be overheard, "Aunt Ada has a very cruel brother."

Brother? thought James.

At that moment, Mrs. Ivan swept back into the room with a rustle of her long, black skirts. Her thin, bony face presided over the tea tray for the next few minutes. Not a hair in the knot at the back of her neck was out of place.

James, who wasn't easily upset, made conversation.

"I see there are some instruments of torture on your walls," he said, pointing to thongs, several whips, a miniature rack, a thumbscrew.

"To remind us of what the holy martyrs suffered in order to be pure," said Aunt Ada Ivan.

"I see," said James. Then, easily changing the subject, he said, "And what are you going to wear to the dance next week, Sasha? The

Rock is coming up on Saturday, you know, Mrs. Ivan — the yearly high school dance."

"Dance?" gasped Mrs. Ivan. "I'd never permit Sasha to go to a dance!"

James and Honey left as soon as they finished their tea. On the way to the car, James said, "I expected that awful woman to object to Sasha's going to the dance."

Honey was so relieved to be out of that house and back in the bright autumn day in the bright red car under the bright Nebraska skies, she felt her heart leap.

"She's certainly a killjoy," she agreed, flinging her long honey-gold hair free in the wind.

"She's more than a killjoy," said James. He gunned the Firebird angrily. As he never mistreated his car, Honey was instantly alert.

"What is it?" she demanded.

It took James a few moments to speak. He drove for a while first, through the town he loved, as always making mental notes of any small changes for ready reference if or when needed.

Red and gold leaves were beginning to fall on the green rectangle at the center of town. From the Green sprang all Kings Rock streets, Northbend and Southbend Avenues going east and west, High Street and Park Street going north and south. To the northwest, at the foot of the Sand Hills, was Rock Bluffs, with the rock plateau called Kings Rock that gave the town its name. To the northeast were the shopping malls, arcades, junk food row, and Loden Airport. To the east was the railroad; to the south of Kings Rock was Summertree River, flowing into Middle Loup River. To the west of town stretched the farms, the cornfields, and the cattle herds of Nebraska.

"I don't like not knowing exactly where everything is," James often said. "Makes me feel out of control."

He drove around the Green twice, past Torello's Hardware Store, Miss Toni's Fashions, and The Hut, where the gang from school ate pizza, played video games, and hung out. He drove past Kings Rock's two movie theaters, past the drugstore, the church, the bank, Pell's Department Store, past the lacy bandstand at the north end of the Green, past the Lion Pride statue at the other end. Then, with a rush, James headed out of town.

For a change, instead of driving northwest

to his favorite place up on Kings Rock, he drove south to Summertree River.

Honey understood. The woods near the river would gentle him down. She sensed some pain in James that he had caught from Sasha, a deeper pain than James usually felt.

They walked silently along Summertree Track, under the willows along the river's edge. The rippling water was calming, and they heard songbirds.

"Those whips aren't there just to remind people about the martyrs," James suddenly said. "In that house, they're used to *make* martyrs."

"You think those whips on the walls were the ones that made the marks on Sasha's back?" Honey asked.

"One of them still had blood on it," said James, his teeth clenched against his rage.

Honey gasped. "We'll get her on child abuse," she said, her rage now as intense as James's. "Let's call Police Chief Frank Adams right away."

James's face darkened. "Even if we got Mrs. Ivan on a child abuse charge, what would happen to Sasha? A foster home? A state institution?"

James, who had been adopted from one,

was sensitive on the subject of state homes for orphaned and abandoned children.

"That's if we could even get Sasha to admit there's no brother, that her Aunt Ada is doing the beating," James went on.

"But why wouldn't she, if she knew she'd be legally protected?" asked Honey.

James sighed. "Most abused children don't know there's a different way to live. When they find out, they often feel it's their own fault somehow that they're being beaten — that they're worse in some way than other children, or that they deserve the beatings. Most of them never want to leave the parent who beats them. Instead they want approval and love and acceptance from the very parent who's been withholding it. They don't realize it's a game they can't ever win."

Honey went pale, as James continued. "Most parents who beat their children were beaten themselves when they were young. By the time they're adults, they're too sick to change without help. Child abuse goes on from one generation to the next."

Honey sat quietly under a tall willow while James talked. She knew he was transferring feelings to thoughts, so they wouldn't hurt so much. James had seen and learned too much about child abuse too early himself. Just pouring out words helped kill the pain he felt for Sasha.

Honey touched James's hand. "What can we do?" she asked softly.

The sun had begun to set. The gold light fired the trees and the water, until the light was more than light, until the light became something so magical it took their breath away. In that light, James's brooding, dark face suddenly lit with joy.

"I've got an idea, Honey," he crowed. "Blast, have I got an idea!"

CHAPTER THREE

"We've Got a Princess, Sam!"

When Sasha fainted outside the locker room the next morning, Honey sent someone to find James. There were no teachers around, and she wouldn't let anyone else touch Sasha. She knew only too well what was the matter.

When James got there, he decided not to waste any more time. He picked Sasha up gently and carried the frail girl outside. Honey followed close behind.

Sasha moaned once or twice.

"Careful of her back, James," Honey whispered.

"I'm being as careful as I can," said James.

James put Sasha into the Firebird. When she was settled, Honey lifted Sasha's gray sweater just a little. There were fresh welts,

even angrier-looking than those of the day before.

Sasha's eyelids fluttered. When she realized she was with James and Honey, she gave a little sigh.

"Yes, that's right, you're safe now," said James. "Sasha, you've got to let us help. I've got a tremendous idea. Will you let me tell you about it? After school?"

"She can't get through school," Honey protested.

"She can't go home either," said James grimly. "And if she goes to the nurse, the nurse will suspect something and call Chief Adams. Not that I'd mind! I'd love nothing better than to hang that old witch! But I don't suppose Sasha would let us. Would you?" he asked.

Sasha had only enough strength to shake her head. There was no way she would accuse her aunt.

Honey smoothed the dark, waving hair back from Sasha's pale face. Then she held out her hand to James for the Firebird's keys.

"I'll take her home until school's over," said Honey. "I mean to my house, James, not hers. Dad's away again. And that one-woman cottage industry, my mother, will be glad of the company."

James nodded his approval. He leaned into the car to touch Sasha's hand.

"I'll come collect both of you after school, then," he said. "Honey's right, Sasha. Her father's always away on one of his oil deals, and her mother rattles around that estate, making everything from pink sweaters to blue baskets. It's my private opinion, she wants a new generation to put in them." James smiled, winked, and ducked Honey's mock tiger-claw lunge.

At three that afternoon, James did the mile run from Kings Rock High School on Park Street South, west on Southbend Avenue, and up the Hill to the Mack Estate.

They all packed themselves into the front seat of the Firebird, and James drove up High Street to Charlie's house. The Alda house was just a couple of doors down from the Star Agency. James parked the car in the alleyway behind High Street, and led the way through Mrs. Alda's hydrangea bushes into the Alda back yard.

"We need Charlie to help with his computer," James explained. "You'll understand my idea in about twenty minutes. Charlie's waiting for us."

Charlie was out back in his shed. His father, supportive of Charlie's genius and a builder in his own right, had built the shed for Charlie to use as a lab for his inventions and for privacy from his five younger brothers and sisters.

"You can understand my gloom about the overcrowded conditions on this planet," Charlie often said over his rocket models. "My own personal experience makes me want to add *any* contribution I can to *any* technology program that would help me to resettle on *any* other planet."

James led Sasha into the shed, which was filled with models of a high-tech space satellite, space station, and rockets as well as the usual lab table of Bunsen burners, tubes, and flasks. On the table near the door was Charlie's great pride and joy. In return for working after school at Torello's Hardware Store, Mr. Torello had sold Charlie his used Apple II for a reasonable price. Besides the 64K computer keyboard and display monitor, there were two disc drives, a printer, and a modem. Charlie was saving for a laboratory data analyzer.

"You ready for us?" James asked.

His favorite part of the Apple II was the modem and its CompuServe connection to data-base information. With CompuServe, Charlie could do everything from track the stock market to get news from the Associated Press wire. What Charlie liked best was electronic mail—he had access to everybody else on the service and all their information. James liked the news bulletins—and being able to use Charlie's computer buddies and their terminals to make any long-distance telephone connection they wanted.

"All ready," said Charlie. He punched a few keys, picked up the modem, and spoke into it.

On the other end, in a capital no one knew much about, located in a tiny principality few people had ever heard of, was Sam Star.

"Charlie's a genius. No missing princess yet. How ya doing?" said Sam. Sam always spoke into the telephone as if he were sending a telegram.

"Fine," said James.

"I want you here in Mornia next weekend," said Sam. "Bring Honey. Charge tickets Lost Princess Account."

"I have a better idea," said James. "Don't look too hard over there. I've got a princess right here for you. I'll bring her over the weekend after next."

"This connection can't be too good," said Sam. "Thought you said you had a princess."

"That's right, Sam. I've got a princess," James shouted into the receiver, and then broke the connection.

He took a deep breath. "That'll give Sam something to think about," said James.

"That'll give *Sam* something to think about?" Honey gasped.

James grinned. He knew Honey realized exactly what he planned to do.

"How are we going to teach Sasha to be a princess in ten days, James Budd?" asked Honey. "That *is* your brilliant idea, isn't it? To get Sasha away from Mrs. Ivan by convincing everyone she's the missing princess of Mornia?"

Sore back or not, Sasha got up from the stool where she had been sitting quietly and listening.

She swept suddenly and gracefully into a deep curtsy. It was so perfect, so courtly, that even the dull gray wool sweater and skirt seemed transformed into a ball gown.

"It's not hard, doing the Missing Princess," said Sasha, raising her eyes demurely, as if she had just been presented at court. "It's not hard at all."

CHAPTER FOUR

Sasha in Trouble

"Are you crazy?"
"You can't do that!"
"What if they find the real princess?"
"You'll never get away with it!"
"Of course we'll help."
"How long have we got?"
The voices echoed around the kung fu practice hall on the Kawabata farm. The Kawabata family had come from Japan to live among the cornfields of Nebraska, where they grew feed crops and dairy cattle. Though their barns and silos were thoroughly American, their home was Japanese, and included meditation and practice halls, a teahouse, and a rock garden. They had brought with them Zen Buddhism, with its beautiful attention to the details of life, its tea ceremony, archery, and the practice of judo,

kung fu, and karate. Tad Kawabata was in James and Honey's class at Kings Rock High, and James and his friends were often at the farm, where Mr. Kawabata gave them all lessons in the martial arts, stressing always its use only in defense, never attack.

They were all here now in the practice hall, in their white kimono jackets and practice trousers. Mr. Kawabata had not yet begun their evening class, and everyone was gathered around James and Honey.

From Charlie's house, James, Honey, Charlie, and Sasha had gone to The Hut for something quick to eat, and then to the library. James and Honey had found some etiquette books and two detailed histories that contained information about the principality of Mornia. They were especially interested in the revolution, and the dispersal and eventual reinstatement of Mornia's royal family.

"We have to teach Sasha everything," said James. "She has to know all there is to know about Mornia, the family history, the Castle Frankovna."

"She's especially got to learn about Princess Tatiana Alexandrovna, the missing princess who's to inherit the throne," said Honey.

"You see, everybody, Sasha is going to *be* the princess, Her Royal Highness, Princess Tatiana Alexandrovna, heiress to the throne of Mornia," said James. "The real princess has been missing since she was a little girl. When the revolution began in Mornia about twelve years ago, the rebels attacked Castle Frankovna, where the royal family lived. The old prince and princess and the three oldest children were taken away and reportedly shot. The youngest, Princess Tatiana, was taken out of the castle in a laundry basket by her nurse. Her people have always believed she survived. And now that the revolution-aries are no longer in power, they want their royal family back. They want to crown Ta-tiana Alexandrovna as Mornia's rightful head of state."

"Such a little place, Mornia, for so much fuss," Sasha murmured. "It was overlooked by all those big countries and left in peace for centuries, like Liechtenstein and Monaco. Now all this fuss. But it's good that the Mornians are free again, isn't it?"

Sasha spoke quietly, but with much feel-ing, as if she had a special empathy with op-pressed people longing for freedom. James, who himself had a passion for freedom, understood.

"So," said James to the others, "you'll help? We need you." He looked around and smiled. He was a loner in many ways, but he knew the value of friends.

Charlie, his cute, owlish face shining behind his horn-rimmed glasses, was the first to volunteer. He was devoted to James and was usually either delighted or panicked when James was around, depending on whether or not James was in danger. He went and stood near James, holding paper and pencil ready to sign people up and make lists.

Tad Kawabata's hand went up next, and then Kathy Howard's.

"If Honey's in this, so am I," said Kathy. "Besides, you'll need help with clothes."

"I will," said Sasha gratefully. "Thank you."

James nodded. He had been worried about whether Sasha would get involved deeply enough for his plan to work. But each time she spoke, James felt her involvement deepen.

Kathy stepped forward and hugged the girl. Kathy herself was tall, elegant, black, and gorgeous. She had three passions in life:

being gorgeous, falling in love often, and astrophysics. Kathy Howard's idea of heaven was to be up in a NASA Spacelab, along with five men, wearing something chic in a spacesuit.

"We'll love it," said Kathy. "Turning you into a princess, I mean."

"We sure will," said Clara Rand, Kings Rock High School's best artist. "The Rock is coming up on Saturday. It will be the perfect time for your coming-out party." The Rock was the big event of the fall semester, the dance for the whole senior high school.

Joe Levy, football hero and dance chairman, came forward. "I'll help you make a grand entrance, if you like, Sasha. We've never had a princess at the Rock before. It'll give us a touch of class," he said, smiling good-naturedly.

Jilly Bruce, their best actress and president of the Drama Club, raised her hand next. "I know something about acting," she said. "I'll be glad to coach you in any scenes you and James think you'll have to get ready for."

"You're all truly marvelous," said James, after everyone in the practice hall had volunteered, "and we're grateful. Now, we haven't much time." He held up the small black-and-white photograph of the princess when she was a little girl. "This is all they know of her—a dark-haired girl of four, with big, sad eyes. The rest, the making of a princess, is up to us—and Sasha."

There was a sudden scuffle at the back of the hall. Joe Levy dragged a small, mean-looking, narrow-eyed, leather-clothed person forward.

"Look what I found listening in," said Joe. "Shall I sit on him for an hour?"

Considering Joe's size, it was an offer of suffocation for Ratso Jones. Trouble for James in Kings Rock came in the form of Ratso and his Rat Gang—his two sidekicks, Tom and Sharky. Ratso's mission in life was to trip up James Budd wherever and whenever possible.

"Must be something worth listening in on, if you're going to all this trouble," said Ratso with a sneer when Joe let him up. He sidled up closer to James. "Anything you'd care to confide to an old friend?"

As Ratso came even nearer, his sidekicks crept forward from the back.

Honey generally got nervous when James

was threatened. She often protected James faster than he needed protection, sometimes even when he needed no protection at all. She could throw a kung fu sunfist punch and do a mean monkey knee. Ratso saw her flick back the long, golden mane, and backed off as she glared down at him warningly.

"Okay, okay," he said, throwing up his hands. "I get the message. But I have my ways of finding things out. I have my ways."

"You just got out of juvenile hall for kidnapping Samantha Smith," said Honey. "With your ways, you'll get right back in."

James simply stood there, examining the weight of his old foe's threat. He wanted no trouble from the old railroad shack.

Ratso's father was the stationmaster, and he had let Ratso and his friends take over an abandoned railroad shack not far from the station. They used it not only as a clubhouse, but for whatever illegal transactions they happened to be planning. James had once or twice seen the medical examiner's report down at the police station on beatings said to have taken place in the Rat Gang's shack. Ratso Jones was no one to have around.

"'Bye for now," said Ratso with a parting

sneer. He threw a quick look at Sasha, as if sensing that she was the center of attention and wondering why. Then he was gone.

"Creep," said Honey.

"Back to schedules?" suggested James, the only one who hadn't turned a hair.

"Nothing ruffles James," said Honey. "Nothing."

Only then something did. From the back of the practice hall came the heavy tread of official feet. Two plainclothesmen arrived, flashed their identification, and stood on either side of Sasha.

"Mrs. Ada Ivan wants the girl. She wants no more interference," said one of the men.

James was more than ruffled. He felt a rare rage. He'd planned a perfect escape for Sasha. Now he had to stand there, watching her being taken away.

CHAPTER FIVE

Royal Family, Royal Hopes

Band-Aid was the neighbors' black Labrador retriever. But it was James whom Band-Aid ran with, slept with, and generally hung out with. At six the next morning, Band-Aid pushed James over in bed, licked his face, and made the throaty sound that, with Band-Aid, passed for conversation.

"Okay, okay," said James. He opened one eye, looked at the clock, and changed his mind. "Not okay, Band-Aid. It's only six in the morning, and breakfast around here is definitely not served before seven-thirty."

Band-Aid pushed, licked, and grumbled again. James sighed, then grew alert. The office telephone downstairs was ringing. He had forgotten to plug in the upstairs extension.

"Thanks, Ban," said James, leaping out of

bed and tearing down the hall, down the front stairs, and through the door to the consultation room.

"Sorry, Sam," said James, interrupting the series of grunts with which Sam indicated he'd prefer not to wait so long for a conversation to begin.

"James, get over here," Sam said after the last grunt. "We're searching every capital, every adoption agency, every orphanage in Europe. Interpol, all the metropolitan police forces, half a dozen private investigators, even a couple of British Intelligence and CIA types—we're all lending a hand. Mornia's cabinet, their prime minister, and the royal family—especially the old dowager, the late princess's sister—all want their princess back. James, we're getting too many letters from too many phony pretenders. Apparently this tiny country has a lot of old money a lot of bigger countries would like to get their hands on, to say nothing of a couple of dozen impoverished barons and out-of-work princes. If Mornia doesn't get the right princess, a lot of wrong people could take over the throne. So, are you coming?"

James hesitated for just a moment. He had

felt a twinge when Sam mentioned phony pretenders. Was that what Sasha would be?

No, thought James, *this is different. We're not trying to steal anyone's fortune. If and when the real princess does turn up, we'll deal with it then.*

"So, are you coming?" Sam repeated.

"Told you, I've got your princess right here," said James, his resolve fully returned. "We'll be over in ten days."

"Why am I having trouble accepting what you're saying?" asked Sam dubiously. "Here I am in Mornia, in the upstairs hall of a fairytale castle, listening to some kid in the middle of Nebraska tell me he's got his hands on a princess to fit into this castle, and I don't believe any of it."

"Talk to the local fairy godmother," said James soothingly. "You'll be all right, Sam. Just hang in there. Be over soon."

James rang off, just a little less sure than he had led Sam to believe. He and Honey had both called the Ivan house several times the night before. No one had answered. They had driven over there. No one had come to the door or acknowledged their knocking.

"Shall we call Chief Adams?" said Honey,

breezing in through the front office just as James got off the phone. "I can't stand to think of Sasha locked up in that house, being beaten over and over."

She threw her tweed jacket onto Sam's leather chair, and began to whip eggs, toast rolls, squeeze orange juice, and make coffee. James followed her into the kitchen, admiring her competence. He knew from past experience that, at the same time as she was doing all of the above, she could also put together a case history, do a chemistry experiment in her head, and give him a kiss without missing a beat.

He cashed in on the last bit. Then he said, "No, sweet. I don't want to bring the chief into this yet if we can help it. I'd rather make a princess than just win a child abuse case that might not even stick. Sasha seems willing to go live her own life, but not to punish her aunt."

"But how do we get to her, James?" Honey asked angrily.

"Don't murder the eggs, my love," said James, taking over the scrambling. "Just coax them around lightly." He produced perfectly scrambled eggs, Honey produced the rolls, coffee, and juice, and they sat down at the kitchen table for breakfast.

"We won't have to get to her," said James. "She'll come back to us. She's brave enough. And besides, there isn't anywhere else for her to go."

James was right. Sasha, with circles under her eyes and walking stiffly, was in school that morning.

"Lunchtime," James whispered during English. "Right here."

By her very silence in the matter, Sasha agreed to show up whenever she could for her lessons.

The first lesson began at noon that day. Almost by an unspoken agreement, neither James nor Sasha mentioned the beatings, the plainclothesmen, Sasha's refusal to prosecute Ada Ivan, or anything else about her present life. They concentrated instead on Sasha's future as the royal princess of Mornia, Her Royal Highness Princess Tatiana Alexandrovna.

"To begin at the beginning," said James, his feet up on one desk, lunch on another— he had brought a thermos and sandwiches for both of them. "You've got to know the history of Mornia. I've found this book. It places Mornia's history neatly in the context of the world's history. Ready?"

Sasha gave a deep sigh. "I've never been madly interested in history," she said.

James laughed. "In this other book Charlie located with his computer at the university library, there are stories about royal families all over Europe. In the story about your family, which you'll have to learn, there's a bit about you as a little girl. There isn't much, because you were only four at the time of the revolution. But you know what it says? It says that the youngest princess, Tatiana, was a bright, lively, intelligent child, but one who would much rather be outdoors running wild than inside at her lessons."

Sasha gave a small laugh, the first James had ever heard her utter.

"It's as if I have the beginning of an identity after all. Oh, James, I wish this were true, that this story were truly about me, that I really did have a family of my own, somewhere I belonged," said Sasha. Her faint European accent lent so much charm to her emotion, James felt for a moment as if he really were helping a princess out from under a wicked spell and back to her own life in her castle. He leaned forward to look into the smoky green eyes, starry for just that moment with hope and pleasure.

Then both of them had a reality attack and went back to the book. Real or not, there was a monumental amount of work to be done.

"Ready?" said James.

"Ready," said Sasha in a determined little voice.

" 'Mornia slipped right through the fingers of the great giants of western history,' " James read. " 'The great nations rose and fell, from the earliest western civilization six thousand years ago, Sumeria, through all the great civilizations around the Mediterranean Sea— Egypt, Israel, Greece, Rome, Byzantium. Then Mornia slipped through the Middle Ages, when the nations of Europe began to form. By the eighteenth century, the European nations were as firm as those of the Far East, whose histories stretched back even farther than those of the West. Germany and Italy gathered themselves in the nineteenth century, and after the Civil War, the United States was finally an undivided nation. South America, which had been conquered by

Europeans, had to regroup entirely. All this upheaval—not to mention the histories of Africa and Australia—and through it all, Mornia simply slipped through, happily overlooked, blissfully ignored.' "

James had to stop, he was laughing so hard. "Did you ever hear anything like it?" he gasped.

"Why is James laughing?" Sasha asked Honey, who had come in during James's reading.

"I don't think either of us has ever read an entire history of the world disposed of so quickly from such a tiny point of view," said Honey. "I mean, here's this little country summing up six thousand years in reference only to itself."

"It is funny at that," said Sasha. But her voice was a little stiff, as if she had been slightly insulted.

"I was also laughing at all the work the world has done to divide itself into nations," said James. "Remember what we were talking about in history today? About how we had better reverse the national process and take the global view that we are all just inhabitants of Earth? Obviously, as long as there are separate nations, they're going to fight. When we stop being separate we'll do what's good for us all. So as I was reading," James added, "I was thinking of the six thousand years worth of effort that had better go down the drain fast. Remember that last case, *The Secret of Operation Brain*, Sasha?"

"Yes, the one Honey wrote up for the *Kings Rock Times*," said Sasha. "You wrote about being one world in that article, Honey, didn't you? You said there's no point in just taking away weapons. If nations went on being divided, they would just make more. I can see that now." Sasha considered the matter quietly and seriously for a moment. "Any head of state ought to work for that," she said.

James exchanged a look with Honey. It wasn't the first time he had heard this responsible tone in Sasha's voice, so different from the lost, frightened little girl.

"You don't suppose . . ." Honey began, looking very hard at Sasha, "you don't suppose you could actually be—I mean—your age is exactly the right age, your coloring is exactly the right coloring, the adoption agency we called said they wouldn't give out any particulars about you—"

"Honey," said James, "you're babbling. I don't say it's nonsense you're babbling. I just say you're babbling."

Sasha had turned pale as Honey spoke. She knew perfectly well what Honey was wondering. The thought was terribly frightening. It was one thing to be trained to be a princess. It was almost a game that way.

It was another thing to begin wondering if you really were.

CHAPTER SIX

Danger in Kings Rock

Today, being Thursday, Sasha had said, was Aunt Ada's church day. Sasha did not have permission to bring friends home, or to visit them. But with Aunt Ada out, Sasha's absence might go unnoticed.

"Of course, she sometimes comes home suddenly to check on me," said Sasha. "But it's the best day to chance it, and I do need so much help if I'm to make you all proud of me."

Honey was moved by Sasha's gratitude for their interest in her. Right after school, she and Kathy, Clara, and Jilly were all going back to the Mack house with Sasha. They stood with James on the front steps of the school, getting organized.

"Here's the etiquette book, and the Mornia history," said James. "The history tells about the royal household—the lord chamberlain, the master of the household, footmen, ladies-in-waiting, the whole castle staff. Especially look up that nanny, the one who was supposed to have smuggled the princess out of the country. Sasha's going to have to know how to address all those people, how they're to address her, all that. Make a beginning there. She seems to know how to curtsy well enough, but check her walk, and Honey, put her in one of those ball gowns your attic is full of, and see how she manages a long train."

Sasha stood by, listening meekly as James gave the orders. "I'll do my best," she promised.

"So will I," said Honey, sighing. "It's an awful lot."

"It'll be an awful lot worse if she's found wanting," said James.

"Heart of stone, that boy," said Kathy, to no one in particular. "It isn't easy learning to walk serenely down a large staircase in full skirts and a train with a crown on your head. But how would he know?" Kathy had won enough beauty contests to know you needed the poise of a trained dancer, the balance of a high-wire artist, and perfect nerves to come down a staircase fully gowned without looking at your feet.

James was beginning to glare.

"But we'll do it, we'll do it, we'll learn, we'll teach Sasha, don't worry," said Jilly. As an actress, not much besides stage fright got to her—except James Budd.

"What about you?" James asked, turning to Clara. "You having problems, too?"

"As a matter of fact, yes," said Clara. "I got your list of clothes I have to design and get made for Sasha. You've got to be crazy, wanting all that in ten days."

"Nine," James corrected Clara coolly.

Then James broke into an affectionate smile, and gave them each a quick hug of encouragement and appreciation.

"He's irresistible," said Honey, "blast him!"

"Right," said James, cool again. "Now, I'll be at Charlie's house. We're working on some new electronic gadgets for the car. If you need me." And he was off.

"Time," said Honey. "Off we go. Sasha, climb on."

Sasha's eyes widened, but she made no

protest. Honey Mack's favorite form of transportation was her blue Honda CB 125S. She handed Sasha the spare helmet, and they were gone.

James drove the Firebird up Park Street and west on Southbend, then out of town on Old Cattle Road. He and Charlie lived only a couple of blocks north of the school, but James wanted to let the car out. Old Cattle Road had no shoppers, or children, or double-parked citizens gossiping peacefully on a lovely October afternoon.

There was no one on the road. James let the Firebird out, enjoying the wind in his face through the open windows, and the freedom of the empty earth and skies.

He got to enjoy all that for approximately five minutes. Then, from out of nowhere, across acres and empty acres of endless Nebraska fields, a big yellow tractor appeared on the horizon. James saw it first in his rearview mirror. It didn't seem to be attending to farm work. It didn't seem to be following any pattern that James could see.

What it seemed to be following, James couldn't help noticing finally, was James.

"I don't believe it," James said, transfixed.

As James went on watching rather than speeding, the tractor got closer.

Moments later, the tractor was close enough for James to see who was trying to pile into him. There on the driver's seat was an amazing-looking man, a man who might have just emerged from a fairy-tale forest. He wore a swirling dark cape lined in red silk, and a wide-brimmed black hat over a red bandana tied pirate-fashion. And he had a great handlebar mustache under which an enormous mouth appeared to be yelling.

"I don't bloody well believe it!" James said again. "Either I've gone mad, or I'm being chased down Old Cattle Road by a crazed gypsy who is about to run me down with a tractor!"

But the tractor was gaining, and a few seconds later it was no joke. James was in no mood to lose either his life or his car. The tractor was on the road now, its massive weight ready to crush the Firebird like an elephant coming down on a toy red wagon.

James pulled ahead. The tractor tore in closer. James needed space for what he had to do. He pulled ahead again. There . . . just enough . . . a little more . . . *now!*

James reached for one of two special buttons on the dashboard. Charlie had installed the two pieces of equipment only a few days before. The first button released enough black oil from two rear pumps to make the road behind James almost undrivable—and it threw the tractor into a spin.

But the gypsy was not about to give up, and James was grateful to Charlie for the second button. He pushed it and careened forward, just as the tractor came out of the spin and was nearly on top of James again.

The second button released two bursts of gray smoke. The smoke fogged the road completely and clouded the gypsy's vision just long enough for James to swerve, cut off Old Cattle Road to the left, and disappear into one of Mr. Kawabata's open cow barns.

Two hours later, James appeared in the huge front hall of the Mack mansion and stood casually at the foot of the stairs, watching a parade of girls coming down the grand formal staircase.

"What an afternoon we've had," said Honey.

"Have you?" said James.

"And you've just been playing with Charlie," said Honey. She mopped her forehead and flung the long golden mane over her shoulders.

"Right," said James. "Me and a gypsy."

As James told the horrified girls how he'd nearly been stampeded by a killer set loose on a tractor, a slow, regally annoyed voice came from the top of the stairs.

"That would be Laszlo. We were told about him as children. He was a hired assassin in the employ of Baron Janos, an enemy of my family."

The voice was Sasha's—yet it wasn't.

The information came from none of the books they'd been reading.

A second later, Sasha came down the staircase, in a full gown and train, with two books on her head, and without a single glance at her feet.

"You have to be taught to walk like this before you are six," she said. "Otherwise, it is too late."

CHAPTER SEVEN
Watching Eyes, Waiting Shadow

Friday lunchtime was Jilly Bruce and Joe Levy's shift. James looked in for a minute at the empty classroom where Sasha continued, on James's orders, to walk about with books on her head while she learned her Mornia lessons.

James had spoken to Sam again that morning. Sam, along with half a dozen other agents, was still trying to trace the nurse who had smuggled the littlest princess over the border and into western Europe for safety.

"My nurse's name was Katerina Fyodorovna. We called her Nanny," said Sasha, moving steadily among the desks, her head held high under its load of books.

"Your parents?" Joe prompted.

"My father was His Royal Highness, Prince Alexander Ivanovich Ivanov," Sasha began. "My mother, Her Royal Highness Princess Sofya Ivanovna. They were cousins, both from the House of Ivanov."

James, standing in the doorway, idly flicking a bit of thread from his perfectly tailored gray slacks, suddenly felt like an idiot. Why hadn't he wondered before whether the name Ada Ivan was connected to the royal house of Mornia? He'd have to get a message to Sam Star quickly, and call Police Chief Frank Adams to see what could be traced from this end.

"My mother's sister, my aunt, the Dowager Princess Anna Ivanovna, my two older brothers Prince Dimitri and Prince Misha, my sister Princess Natasha—"

"Better remember their full names, Sasha," Jilly said.

In Mornia, the formal greeting included both the given name and the patronymic—a middle name taken from the father's name. Less formally it was just the given name or a nickname. Her own name, Sasha, was the nickname for Alexandra—or Alexandrovna, the patronymic for a daughter of Alexander.

Sasha repeated the names in full.

"And the names of the staff? The members

of the prince's household?" Joe prompted.

Sasha went on. "The sergeant footman who sent all the pages running was Grigory." She smiled as she spoke Grigory's name. "And everyone called Nanny by her nickname, Katya. She always wore blue. We used to run away from her, across the green lawns and into the forest to hide. It made her crazy."

For a moment Sasha's pale, haunted look was gone, and the face of a happy young girl took its place. Where, James wondered, had she gotten these stories of Princess Tatiana's childhood? Not from the books they had gotten out of the public library. Were there other books about Mornia, perhaps on the shelves of Ada Ivan's house? Had Sasha read the stories when she was younger and identified with them to brighten her awful life with Ada Ivan?

Or was there an even deeper mystery, a more serious truth?

Suddenly a different sound came from Sasha, breaking into James's thoughts.

"James, I can't. I can't do this. I can't turn into a storybook princess for you, I can't. I can't! My mind is swimming with all those names and all the histories. I'm frightened.

Let me go back to the life I know," Sasha wailed. She took the books from her head and set them on the nearest desk with a bang. "I'm tired. I can't do it. I can't go on with this."

Then she burst into tears and collapsed onto the chair, burying her head in her arms.

James strode coolly across the room and stood in front of her.

"Tatiana Alexandrovna, stand up, put the books back on your head, and go on with your lessons," he said. "Joe, go over every family name and every member of the royal household again. Jilly, go over the descriptions of the castle, the rooms, the jewelry, the court clothes. If she ends up forgetting something, it can be attributed to her being so young at the time of the revolution or her nanny's forgetting to tell her the story. If she knows too much, or seems too studied, it can be blamed on her very great interest in her own country, so natural to someone who is someday to be a head of state. Don't stop for a minute."

Joe and Jilly stared at James's unbending back as he strode from the room.

Sasha, however, swept regally to her feet and calmly continued her lessons.

As often as Sasha broke down—and in between the joy she seemed to feel when she spoke of life in the castle, she often did break down—James either quietly ordered her to go on or yelled at her.

That evening, as he and Honey did the coaching in the living room of the Star Agency, he yelled twice.

Once was to say, "You've said you want to belong somewhere, to have a real family."

"I do," wept Sasha. "I do, more than anything."

"Then work!" yelled James. "You've got to pass a close examination by people who knew you, knew your family. Your parents and brothers and sister may be dead, but a lot of the staff is alive. The prime minister is alive. And hardest of all, your dowager aunt is alive. Don't you think they're going to be hard on you, pry into every corner of your mind? So we must be just as hard, harder, on you here. You must be perfect, do you understand? You're not going to inherit a throne unless you *are*, not just seem to be, Her Royal Highness the Princess Tatiana Alexandrovna."

The second time James yelled was at ten o'clock, when Sasha pleaded fatigue.

"Your Aunt Ada won't be home from church until eleven," said James. "That gives us another half-hour. Address everyone properly one more time."

"No, I won't," said Sasha.

"Yes, you will," yelled James.

Sasha went through the proper forms of formal address from royalty to footmen one more time.

Finally everyone, not just Sasha, was exhausted and drained. "Tomorrow's the dance," said Honey. "Can you come over to my house to try on gowns in the afternoon? Kathy and I are going to raid the attic."

Even though rock, disco, and country-and-western were going to be played, the girls had decided to dress up for the Rock. It was fortunate. It would give Sasha a chance to spend the evening in the kind of clothes she would have to wear for her presentation at court—if Sam could get her a presentation.

On Saturday afternoon, while the girls took Sasha up to the Mack attic to dig through old trunks and wardrobes for clothes, James took a moment for himself. He needed to think. He got into the Firebird and drove north into the country on Old Cattle Road.

James could see Kings Rock from his bedroom window, hear the wind sweep and moan across it from the mountain pass. The high outcrop had the color, the roar, and in bad weather the treachery of an angry lion, the king of beasts—hence its name.

It was James Budd's favorite place. Few other people went there at all. No one ever followed him.

As James went up from the prairies and into the hills that afternoon, the windswept rock, spare but for brush and scrub trees, cleared his head. It was cold, but he had brought a thermos of coffee, and his down jacket was warm.

The afternoon sun spread a glittering light across the empty sky, and James waited for answers to his unspoken questions to come from the shining air.

With all the good will in the world, his mind said, *I'm playing with someone's life. I'm taking a beautiful young girl who just might survive the dreadful life she's got now, and pushing her into a test that could break her heart if all doesn't go well.*

No answer came from the mountain skies—but a knife did. As it narrowly missed James's ear, he spun in the direction from

which it had been flung. The branches of a scrub oak above moved just barely, but enough for James to see a shadowy figure slip from the tree to behind an enormous boulder above James's head.

James was fast. The knife-thrower was just as fast. A second knife came hurtling down at James within seconds after the first.

CHAPTER EIGHT

James Is Kidnapped

James held Honey close to him on the dance floor, as the band slowed from rock to a ballad and the lights dimmed.

"One of us has enemies," James said into the honey-gold hair soft against his cheek. "I love you."

Honey clung to the dark, handsome young man, stunning in a tuxedo and white evening shirt. She looked up at him as adoringly as he looked down at her, slender and beautiful in a simply cut, dusky blue gown. Elegant, close, perfectly in step, they were splendidly matched as they moved over the dance floor.

James's breath caught in his throat. He needed little in his life, but he needed this girl to share his adventures, his passion for excitement, his love.

"I love you, too," Honey whispered back,

her eyes shining into his. "One of who has enemies?"

James laughed. His girl never missed a beat.

"Either Sasha—or I."

James told Honey about the knife-throwing incident up on Kings Rock, and about the shadowy figure he felt watching him then— and since.

"If Mr. Kawabata hadn't taught us how to respond to surprise attack," James said, "I'd have been wearing something trendy in bandages tonight."

Honey shuddered at the possibility.

"The worst of it is the feeling I'm still being watched," said James. "I still feel eyes on me, a presence somewhere in the shadows, waiting."

"That gypsy, the one that Sasha mentioned the other day, what was his name?" asked Honey.

"Laszlo, the gypsy assassin hired by Baron Janos, the royal family's enemy," James answered. "Yes, it might have been Laszlo. But since I saw only a shadow, I can't be sure. I'm only sure that we have a knife-thrower in our town who could have an interest in this affair.

It wouldn't be the first time Ratso Jones, for instance, accepted a fee to drop out of a tree on my head."

"You mean Laszlo might have been approached by Ratso already?" said Honey.

"Or by someone else," said James. "Ratso has some awful connections. Anyone who wants a local goon can find the Rat Gang. There might be other interests who want the lost princess not to be Sasha. Sam said there were a whole lot of pretenders to the throne of Mornia."

Honey stopped dancing mid-step.

"Not like ours," she said. "Look, James. Look at ours. Look at her!"

Many other couples also stopped dancing and fell away as Sasha Ivan came through the open double doors into the ballroom. A lot of work had turned the gym into a fairyland. The walls and ceiling were draped with yards of pale gauze, chandeliers were hung, the stage was turned into an old-fashioned bandstand.

Now into this fairyland came not just another girl in an evening dress, but a young woman transformed. Sasha entered the ballroom wearing a white satin gown with a long train, Mrs. Mack's small diamond tiara, and a white satin cape lined in brilliant red silk. She carried a small bouquet of white roses, and her other hand rested lightly on the arm of Joe Levy, her prince escort for the evening. Charlie Alda, eyes glowing behind the horn-rimmed glasses, was just behind, footman and driver.

James was instantly impressed. There was more here than a beautiful girl dressed up in evening clothes borrowed from friends. Sasha Ivan had a presence so regal it filled the room. Watching her, James felt certain that someone, somewhere, very early in Sasha's life, had implanted in her a specialness, an apartness, a sense of authority that had never left her, despite the hardships and humiliations of her life.

All it had taken from James and Honey was the suggestion that Sasha might be Her Royal Highness Princess Tatiana Alexandrovna. This exquisite, royal presence in the ballroom was the result.

James moved slowly toward Sasha. He stopped a few feet before her, bowed, then extended his hand. Almost on cue, the band played something slow, and James led their princess in her first dance. A hush fell over the crowd. It was as if they were in an eighteenth-century ballroom watching the prince and princess have the first waltz. In another moment, Joe extended his hand to Honey, Tad to Jilly, David Rivera to Kathy Howard. The dance returned to normal then. But no one could forget those first spellbinding moments when Sasha had entered the room.

"She made magic," said Honey when she and James had returned to each other. "Sasha made magic happen."

"I wish she could make the same kind of magic happen at home with her Aunt Ada," said James grimly. "Mrs. Ivan granted a rare favor when she gave Sasha permission to visit you and your mother this evening.If she ever finds out that Sasha came to the Rock, I hate to think what Sasha's punishment might be."

The punishment came swiftly. It happened so fast there wasn't a thing James could do about it.

Aunt Ada suddenly appeared in the doorway. Gaunt, powerful in her rigid fury, dressed in black from head to toe, her mouth drawn back as grimly as her hair, she looked like an avenging demon.

Without a word to anyone, she made straight for Sasha. Her strong hands gripped Sasha's arms. The pale ice-blue of her eyes pierced Sasha, as if Sasha were a walking sin.

"Blast," James muttered to Honey. "Blast, blast, blast! I could deck that woman. But if I did, there would be trouble. And we don't want any trouble before we can get Sasha to Europe."

Honey's eyes filled with tears as she watched Sasha being dragged out the door by Ada Ivan.

"James, she's going to be whipped again," Honey whispered. "I can't bear it."

"I only hope Sasha can," said James in a rage. "I only hope she can bear it one more time. If I can help it, it will be the last. Wait here while I go call Sam and see if we can leave sooner than next weekend. I know Sam has a rule that our work must never interfere with school. But Sasha being at the mercy of that woman—that's just too much. I've got to make Sam see reason. I'll be right back."

James left the room and strode down the dimly lit corridor toward the public telephones. He never reached them. An arm encircled his throat, a hand covered his nose with chloroform-soaked cotton, and a huge tarp was thrown over his body.

James felt himself being thrown over a shoulder. Then everything went black.

CHAPTER NINE

Escape to Mornia

When James came to, he was in darkness.

"Golden Rule Number Six," James said into the black room—he made up his Golden Rules as he went along. "Never get caught up in feeling like a knight in shining armor—it makes for cockiness, carelessness, and claustrophobia."

As he spoke, James moved cautiously about in widening circles. He was checking out his surroundings, feeling what he could not see. As he felt his way about, he analyzed the situation.

"Whoever brought me here knows very little about the drug he used," James began. "It wore off faster than he thought, or he'd have tied me up. He's not, then, a professional assassin—unless Baron Janos's Laszlo is more stupid than I thought."

James's hands told him he was in a cement-floored room with no furniture, some trunks and boxes stacked against the walls, a heavy door.

"A cellar, a storeroom—" he went on. Stacking boxes on top of each other, he climbed until he could feel the ceiling. "Normal ceiling, no soundproofing, cobwebby, cement blocks." He climbed down and began to pace the room for size. "Too big for an ordinary basement, and not any of the institutions I've been in before, like the library or police station or City Hall—" James had lived in Kings Rock nearly all his life. He had played in every yard and in most people's cellars, had run every road, walked every street, shopped in all the stores, climbed all climbable trees, explored every hill, river, and bluff, looked under nearly every rock. "By process of elimination, this has to be the only basement conforming to these specifications I know," finished James. "I'm in the railway station storage basement."

James automatically brushed off his hands and the sleeves of his tuxedo jacket.

"Even in the dark of some unknown jungle, at the center of a stampede, James's clothes would be unruffled," Honey once complained.

"Stands to reason that Ratso Jones had a hand in this," James continued. "I'd have been able to kick out the door of the shack. Here, he figured I'd have to stay until come for."

The trouble, James knew, was that Ratso Jones and his goons Tom and Sharky could get nasty with rubber hoses. James had seen the victims of their work not walk for two weeks. James didn't have two weeks. Sasha couldn't last two weeks, with Ada Ivan's beatings coming daily now.

Suddenly there were footsteps, first above James's head, then coming down stairs James knew must be behind the door he had felt across the room.

When whoever was coming down the stairs entered the room, the light switch that had to be outside the door would be switched on. James did not want to be caught awake in the middle of the room in a sudden flood of light.

He was grateful he had regained consciousness in time to explore the room before his visitors arrived. He made a calculated leap and landed behind where the door had to open, seconds before it did.

With him he had carried the heaviest trunk he could lift.

"I've wanted James Budd alone in a dark place, all to myself, for ten years." The sneering voice of Ratso Jones preceded his entrance. "They won't find him here for days."

"Right, Ratso," said Sharky in a guttural whisper a ghoul would have been proud to possess. "We'll hurt him bad and leave him to suffer worse." James could hear the *whoosh* of rubber hose through the air.

Ratso and his goons stood inside the open door for a couple of seconds before switching on the fluorescent lights. Those few seconds gave James just enough time.

As the lights flickered on, James took a swift step forward, then brought the trunk crashing down. He got Ratso's head and Tom's shoulder. Sharky leaped clear, spun, and made a grab for James, already part way up the stairs.

His rubber hose caught James's thigh

rather painfully. But James's kung fu round kick to Sharky's temple spun Sharky ten feet back through the air and down to the cement floor.

"You're limping," said Honey an hour later.

"You're kidding," said James, wincing up the columned entrance to the Mack mansion.

"James," Charlie called out from the hall, "that you? I brought Honey home when you didn't come back to the dance. I've been calling everywhere. What happened?"

James briefly replayed his past couple of hours. Then he said to Charlie, "We need your Apple. Can you get us through to Sam fast? And make some reservations fast?"

"Whatever," said Charlie.

Under the circumstances, even Sam agreed to waive the rule about never missing school. "Don't need a battered princess on presentation night," he said.

"To say nothing of my own condition," said James dryly.

"To say nothing," said Sam, with, if possible, even less emotion.

Getting Sasha was easy, if horrible. She was out in the potting shed, chained to a

chair. Only royal blood, thought James, re-
leasing Sasha and seeing the marks on her
back, could account for her not screaming as
he carried her out of the shed, through the
hedge, and into the waiting Firebird. Honey
never stopped trembling until they got to
Loden Airport.

All three felt better once they were on the
plane for New York, where they would con-
nect for Europe. They would fly first to Paris,
change planes for Budapest, capital of
Hungary, and from there fly to a town whose
name only Sasha could pronounce, Nyíregyháza. There they would meet Sam and drive
northeast to Mornia.

"You all right?" Honey asked the pale,
frightened girl.

"I'm grateful for all you've done," said
Sasha, hunched between James and Honey.

Honey had found some new clothes for
Sasha in an airport shop, and had taken her
into the women's room. There she had
bathed the girl's back as well as she could,
covered the angry red welts with a soft tee-
shirt, then dressed her for the long journey.

James looked into Sasha's face and saw
none of the regal strength with which she

had swept into the ballroom at school the night before. James left the gentle sympathy to Honey. His own response was sterner stuff.

"We'll occupy ourselves during the flight by going over court protocol," he said. "We'll review the history of Mornia and your family. We'll go over every known detail of your childhood."

"I can't do it, James," Sasha sobbed softly. "I don't even know who I am any more. Sometimes I feel like plain Sasha Ivan. Sometimes I feel as if I really am Princess Tatiana Alexandrovna, as if her memories are my memories, her life my life. And sometimes—sometimes I don't feel like anybody at all, as if I had died years ago, as if I don't belong anywhere, to anyone. I'm just so tired—and so frightened."

James paid no attention to Sasha's grief. As Sasha buried her head in her hands, he only said, "We'll work now, Sasha. Begin with the proper address for your dowager aunt, Anna Ivanovna."

The trip was long. The flights to New York, Paris, and Budapest were smooth. Sam had made certain their papers were all arranged

and waiting for them in Paris. At least there
were no hitches there.

It was on the flight to the Hungarian border, to the town of Nyíregyháza, that James
felt the first sign of trouble. It was a recur-
rence of the feeling of being watched, shad-
owed, by someone behind them on the
plane.

The second sign of trouble, far more visible, came when the three stepped from the
plane.

There was Sam Star, waiting for them as
planned.

Only, not as planned, Sam was surrounded
by guards.

CHAPTER TEN

The Run from the Castle

Sam was James's hero, the one man for whom James would have given his life without hesitation. Seeing him standing there, gray fedora cocked back, between those two bulky men, moved James's feet so fast, he was by Sam's side in seconds, hands ready to strike.

"Hi," said Sam.

"Hi?" asked James. "*Hi?*"

"Meet the palace guard," said Sam. "Give them all your papers. They'll get us through customs. Car's waiting. Hi, kid," he said to Honey, and, seeing Sasha, "She doesn't look like much."

James shook his head slightly and relaxed his fists, let out his breath. Sam had been away on cases so much recently, James had almost forgotten his casual, curt manner.

"Sam, you have no eye for girls, you never did," said Honey. "Sasha, don't be upset. Wait till Sam sees you in a tiara and gown."

Sasha came forward, her hand extended tentatively. Her regal manner had vanished. She once again had the look Honey and James had first seen, the terrified look of an abused little girl.

Honey encircled the dark-haired girl with her arms, trying to soothe the haunted fear out of the smoky green eyes.

James pulled Honey away, almost roughly.

"Tatiana Alexandrovna, your escort is waiting. Give them their instructions," ordered James.

It was as if James's words triggered a long-buried reflex in the girl.

"I am tired. You may bring the car," came the soft, clear, commanding voice. The hand extended to Sam Star lifted slightly in expectation.

Sam's reflexes were equally quick. He bent over the hand of their princess-to-be in a brief salutation, and they all followed the once-more regal girl to the waiting limousine.

"Better," said Sam.

The drive from Nyíregyháza northeast to the tiny principality of Mornia was long but beautiful, taking them through green forests and fields, then along the Tisza River. Willows and birches, tall elms and oak trees overhung the river and the road with the golds and reds of fall.

"It's fairy-tale country," breathed Honey.

When they arrived in Mornia, late in the afternoon, Honey was even more convinced that they had left the world of reality for something out of Andersen or Grimm. The tiny country was full of tidy houses, perfectly shaped fields, trees so tall they arched like cathedrals over the roads. As they drove up the long mall that approached the castle, Honey gasped.

Before them rose the towers and turrets of the royal castle of Mornia. The walls were white with arched windows, the towers were capped with jade-green points and the spires with golden balls. The crenelated fortifications were patrolled by brilliantly costumed guards.

Around the castle stretched what seemed like miles of lawn, and beyond that were green forests and a great, sky-blue lake.

The limousine clattered over the moat's drawbridge and into the vast courtyard of the castle. When it pulled to a stop, Sasha uttered the first words she had spoken in an hour. As she spoke, James could see that she had once more shrunk in fear into herself.

"Am I to—meet anyone? Must I be presented to—anyone? Must it be right away?"

"They're expecting us," Sam told James. "Sasha is one of several young women being brought this week to meet the old dowager and the prime minister and a few of the old guard who remember the princess as a child. It's general inspection time."

"But today?" Sasha's voice was pleading. "Can't there be more time?"

"I'll get you what time I can," said Sam. "But we've been given only two days. Our schedule is to meet the immediate family, the prime minister, and some of the old family friends this evening. If they approve, if they think there is the remotest chance our Sasha meets any of the requirements, then tomorrow an audience with the dowager princess, Anna Ivanovna, will be arranged."

"But we've had such a long journey. Sasha is so tired," said Honey. "They have to give her a chance to do her best, Sam."

"I think their feeling is, either she is Her Royal Highness Princess Tatiana Alexandrovna or she isn't," said Sam. "No amount of time is going to change that."

"But Sasha was such a little girl when she left Mornia," said Honey. "Her confusion and fear would be natural."

"What would we do without Honey's heart, eh, James?" said Sam.

As they spoke, their bags were removed from the limousine. They were then escorted into the largest single room James had ever seen. Statues of armored knights stood on deep, red carpeting along the gold and white walls of the vast front hall. Chandeliers hung from a ceiling that seemed a hundred feet high. The four climbed a high, wide stairway to a balconied hall and were led into a large pale-blue and gold drawing room.

James and Honey watched Sasha's eyes search out every detail with a kind of passionate hunger, as if she were looking at something she had long yearned to see.

"Is she coming home, do you think, James?" whispered Honey. "Or is she only wishing she were?"

"From this moment on," said James, "we are going to assume Sasha is Princess Tatiana

Alexandrovna. We are going to call her that, treat her like that, and just cross our fingers."

Sam had left the three young people for a moment. When he came back he said, "No go. Our young lady is to be presented to the prime minister and the others this evening as scheduled."

Sasha, who had been looking out the high double French windows at the expanse of lawn and the forest beyond, turned slowly.

"It will be all right, James," she said. "But I wish to go riding first. The habits used to be kept in the second attic of the east tower. If someone will fit us out, I remember the stables and the forest."

James refused to register surprise.

"Can you arrange it, Sam?" he asked.

In less than an hour, James, Honey, and Sasha were streaming across the lawn dressed in old-fashioned riding clothes. Honey was in dark green velvet, Sasha in dark, royal red velvet, James in black. Their horses were spirited and ready for a good run.

"I don't believe this," Honey gasped, her long gold hair flying like a banner in the wind.

As they entered the cool forest, they felt like shouting with the joy of being free and outside in the glorious late afternoon.

Suddenly James halted his black stallion.

"Quiet," he ordered. "We were followed on the plane. We were evidently followed here. We are still being followed. I can feel it."

"Oh, James," Honey began to protest. But she stopped when the arrows came.

CHAPTER ELEVEN

Gypsy Arrows
in the Back

The rushing flight of arrows terrified the horses. They reared and bolted, cutting off Honey's words and proving that James's instincts were right, as usual. The three were not only being followed, but shot at.

James and Honey were excellent riders, having roamed the Nebraska plains and hills on horseback since they were small. But if they were good riders, Sasha was superb. Her gelding reared and fled through the forest in the golden light of the late afternoon. She remained in perfect control.

"Follow me," Sasha cried.

Honey's roan settled down enough to obey Honey's directions. James's black stallion continued to rear and plunge—more in fury, it seemed to James, than in panic.

"It isn't you who's been insulted," shouted James, "it's me. Now get us out of here!"

The stallion responded to James's voice and finally plummeted through the forest after Honey and Sasha. Under, sometimes through, the gold-flecked branches of the ancient oaks, the three horses and their riders raced onward.

The arrows pursued them through the trees. Whoever was following them had to be mounted, had to be not only a brilliant horseman but a brilliant archer.

The three horses were now close enough and, despite their speed, calm enough for James and Honey and Sasha to shout to each other.

"There may be more than one," Sasha called to James. "Do you remember the gypsy assassin I told you about? The man called Laszlo? The one Baron Janos used to hire to do his dirty work?"

"I remember," said James over the wind.

"That man Laszlo was the best horseman, the best archer, the most remarkable hunter in all middle Europe."

"How about his knife-throwing?" said

James, remembering the incident at Kings Rock.

"Perfection, of course," Sasha shouted.

As she shouted, her horse sprang over a fallen branch. Excellent horsewoman though she was, Sasha couldn't control the feet of her mount.

"James," Honey yelled. "Sasha's been thrown! James! I can't turn back. Can you get her?"

"Keep going! I've got her," James yelled back.

James reined his black stallion and raced back to where Sasha lay crumpled on the ground.

The archer must have witnessed the accident as well. Just as James reached down to scoop Sasha from the ground and fling her over his saddle, another half-dozen arrows screamed past. One of them nearly nicked the side of James's head.

"Blast!" he shouted. But he controlled his anger. Anger clouded judgment, and he needed no distorted vision here, no emotion, only smooth, clean action. "Where to?" he asked Sasha, who had now righted herself and rode before James in the saddle.

She pointed straight ahead to the edge of the forest and the rising of a green hill. James, now followed by Honey, raced for it.

"To the left," Sasha said.

They rode to the left.

They could now hear the hooves of their pursuer's horse close behind them. He emerged from the trees just as James, Sasha, and Honey started up the hill.

"Faster," said Honey over the rising wind. "He's gaining!"

Sasha led them to the mouth of a cave in the side of the hill. Its entrance was covered with brush. They were off the horses and into the cave in seconds.

"She had to have been here before to know about this," said Honey. "This proves she really is the princess, doesn't it? Doesn't it, James?"

James looked at Sasha. For a moment Sasha looked as surprised as her friends, not certain herself where she had found the memory of this cave.

"It proves nothing," said a voice behind them. "It proves nothing at all. This girl can never inherit the throne of Mornia. It belongs to another. It belongs to the niece of Baron Janos. The baron has worked many years to secure the kingdom for her. When he discovered that Katya, the nurse, had smuggled Princess Tatiana out of the country, he began to train his niece to rule. The young baroness knows now how to rule. She will make a much better ruler than some young, untrained girl who grew up in the United States, in another world far away."

James stepped forward to protect the girls. The assassin stood there in the opening of the cave, large and menacing in his wide dark hat and billowing cape, blocking their exit and any escape into the light of day.

"Tell me, Laszlo—if that is your name," James began.

"That is my name," the gypsy said with pride.

"Tell me, was it Baron Janos who arranged for Princess Tatiana to be taken to the United States and kept away from the throne of Mornia so he could control your country through his niece?"

"Exactly," said Laszlo. "We never knew precisely what happened to the girl. We only sent money to the dead Princess Sofya's sister, Ada Ivanovna, to arrange matters so that Princess Tatiana would never return."

"No," said Sasha in a soft, stricken voice.

"Then she never loved me at all, as she once said she did. Never at all."

"Sasha—Tatiana—dear," Honey said gently. "She may have, only she herself was so sick. And you were in the orphanage for a few years at first. Ada Ivan had to find you, and she may have loved the little girl she found."

While Honey comforted Sasha as best she could, James stood before the powerful gypsy, waiting for his chance.

It came suddenly, unexpectedly. After his long chase halfway across the world and back, Laszlo was so proud to bring the chase to an end, that he threw back his head and laughed, crowed like a rooster bringing up the sun in the morning.

In that split-second James brought Laszlo to the ground.

The three climbed over the unconscious Laszlo, returned to the castle, and, after a long talk with Sam, dressed for the evening's presentation. The cabinet, the prime minister, all the castle staff who remembered, and, except for the dowager princess, whatever family members remained were waiting in the blue and gold drawing room to meet and question Sasha.

Flanked by James, Honey, and Sam, Sasha entered the drawing room in a pale rose chiffon dress, white gloves, and the small tiara she had worn to the dance.

As she rose from her first curtsy to the prime minister and looked up into his eyes, Sasha heard the old man say:

"She will never do, never at all."

CHAPTER TWELVE

The Handsome Prince

James tensed, but it didn't seem to him that Sasha was crushed by the instant rejection. He saw her tremble a little, then rise from her curtsy.

"I'm sorry you feel that way," said Sasha, "I'll try to do better, Your Excellency."

Not only James, but the prime minister was a little impressed by Sasha's presence of mind.

"She's going to try, James," said Honey, delighted with her friend's courage in the face of so immediate a disappointment.

"We knew it wouldn't be easy," James whispered back, "but I'm counting on two things."

"What?" said Honey, as they moved forward to follow Sasha along the reception line in front of the glorious high French windows of the drawing room.

"I'm counting on Sasha's spunk. She's got a lot of that," said James.

"And?" said Honey, curtsying to the prime minister, then to the second duke of Frankovna.

"And," said James simply, "that she is, in fact, the Princess Royal, Tatiana Alexandrovna of Mornia."

Sasha moved with regal grace along the line of little old counts, elderly countesses, young baronets and earls. James could hear Sasha murmur the appropriate greetings.

"Good evening, Your Grace. I'm glad to see you again, Your Eminence. Thank you, Countess Elisabeta Petrovna," and even, "How is your poor back these days, Sir Nicholas?"

When the three young people, and Sam Star, who was right behind them, had come through the last of the reception line, a chair was placed in the center of the drawing room for Sasha. Here she was to sit for an hour or so while anybody who wished to question her might ask the young pretender to the throne of Mornia anything at all.

"At the end of the grilling," said Sam out of the corner of his mouth, "they're going to vote. Poor kid!"

James nodded. "It's rough, but it's what she was intended for, Sam, to handle people like this—her own people."

"You're right about that," said Sam. "If she can't handle this, she'll never be able to rule the country. Mornia may only be a few hundred square miles, but it's bordered by some heavy-hitting countries—Russia, Hungary, and Czechoslovakia. She's got to be able to cope with international politics as well as a drawing room full of old nobility."

"What do you think, James?" Honey asked anxiously. "How is she doing?"

The three stood to one side, balancing teacups and small plates of tiny cakes. They watched Sasha bend politely toward this one, graciously toward that one, in response to a question. As James listened intently, he watched carefully for attitudes. He wanted to hear which duke asked his questions sympathetically, which countess veiled an insult with her remarks, to see which earl or baroness smiled with pleasure, eagerly greeting their lost princess, and which lord or lady sneered because of loyalties placed elsewhere.

"Hard to tell, so far," said James.

"Yes, of course I remember the tennis

games on the lawn on Sunday afternoon, and the music," he heard Sasha say in answer to a question about her childhood. "My sister, Princess Natasha, always lost, and then she would run inside and cry. My two brothers, Prince Dimitri and Prince Misha, always laughed and teased poor Natasha. How she hated that!"

As Sasha spoke, James saw that her eyes were filled with joy, as if these memories were very real and precious to her.

"Either you are a very good actress," said an old countess, "or you are truly Tatiana. Your sister never cried in public, only later on in the privacy of your nursery. You would have to have been there, to know how Natasha cried when she lost at anything."

"Not necessarily," retorted the prime minister. "Ada Ivanova could have told her stories."

"Aunt Ada never told me any of these things," said Sasha firmly. "How could she, when she was paid never to mention my home or my family or my birthright to me at all?"

"That's true," said the second duke of Frankovna.

So it went on, questions and answers, ill-natured sometimes, but always handled by Sasha with firmness, good will, and, James thought, a great deal of royal dignity and self-confidence.

At last the prime minister decided it was time for the voting to begin.

"We must decide whether Sasha Ivan is the true Royal Princess of Mornia or not," said the important old man, patting his bright blue sash of the Order of the Star. "We must weigh carefully her answers to our questions. But more important, we must weigh our own responses, our own smallest intuitive reactions to this young woman. Often, the sense of royalty lies not so much in protocol, but in some inner quality that can only be inherited, never learned. Consider carefully, every one of you. Grigory, hand out the ballots."

Grigory, the aging footman who had been smiling at Sasha whenever he could do so discreetly, came forward to pass out small ivory cards and gilt pencils so that all present might cast their votes.

"Good evening, Grigory," said Sasha, bowing slightly and smiling at the beloved companion of her childhood.

"Good evening, Your Royal Highness," said Grigory. His acceptance of Sasha was absolute.

"Thank you, Grigory," Sasha said warmly.

So far, she had not looked over at Sam and James and Honey. While the court voted, she stole a look. Honey beamed at her encouragingly, Sam nodded and grinned, James looked hard and intently into her eyes. Sasha nodded, and returned her gaze to what was happening in the room.

Suddenly two new figures entered through the arched double doors to the west of the drawing room. A tall young man accompanied a tiny woman in a long, high-necked, black velvet dress. The tiny woman wore her white hair in a topknot, encircled by a small diamond crown.

Sasha rose in a flash and was across the room before anyone could stop her. She fell to her knees before the old woman, burst into tears, and cried out.

"Aunt Anna, Aunt Anna, Aunt Anna, it's me, Sasha. Don't you know me? Please tell me you know me, please let me come home."

The room froze into silence at Sasha's wild outburst.

"Get up, young woman, whoever you are," came the crisp, commanding tones of the dowager princess, Anna Ivanovna. "How dare you make such a public display?"

The tall young man was slender, elegant, finely dressed. He had a strong, chiseled face, with kind eyes and a gentle smile. As he bent over the kneeling Sasha and lifted her to her feet, James heard the dowager princess speak his name.

"Prince Stanislaus, do not interfere. I know that when you were children, you adored Tatiana Alexandrovna. I know that when you were children, you were betrothed in marriage, and that you have never forgotten her, never looked at another girl. But I do not yet know whether this young pretender is just another lie, another paste Tatiana. I wish neither of us to be hurt again by a false hope in another false princess. Let the girl be."

James moved forward. In all his research, he hadn't come across the mention of a prince or a betrothal. He had been unable to coach Sasha about this. She was unprepared. How would she handle this new piece of information?

Prince Stanislaus didn't pause for a moment. As he unhesitatingly gave Sasha his arm in support, his gaze never left her face, his glance never faltered.

"Good for the boy prince," muttered Sam approvingly.

"Cross your fingers," Honey whispered in return. "Maybe if Prince Stanislaus believes Sasha is Tatiana, he can help convince everybody else."

But if the prince had been staring at Sasha, so had the old aunt, equally seriously, equally intently. In the next moment, the commanding voice spoke again.

"It is not necessary, the rest of you, to vote," she said. "I have made up my mind."

CHAPTER THIRTEEN

A Real Princess?

"No, please, give me another chance," James could barely hear Sasha whisper. For the look on the old dowager's face was clear.

"I don't mean to be unkind," said the dowager princess. "It's just that you aren't my Sasha. You are a nice, dear girl. But you're not my niece."

There were sad protests from those who liked and believed Sasha, there were smirks from those who didn't. And there was such bleak loss on Sasha Ivan's face that Sam Star's heart, James saw, couldn't take it. Sam stepped forward.

"Your Highness," said Sam. "Might we request a private audience for Sasha? After all, we've come so far, and Sasha has gone through so much. Perhaps just half an hour with Your Highness would only be fair."

The dowager princess looked up at the famous detective with just a twitch of a smile.

"It is unheard-of to argue with me, young man," she said.

"It is unheard-of to refer to a beat-up party like myself as a young man," said Sam, "but I thank you."

"James," Honey gasped quietly, "he's flirting with her. Sam is flirting with the dowager princess of Mornia."

"You're absolutely right, Honey. And he's got her," said James, his tension dissolving in laughter.

"Very well," the whole room heard Anna Ivanovna say. "Half an hour."

The dowager princess was accompanied by a lady-in-waiting. James was permitted to accompany Sasha. The four, led by the tiny, commanding figure of the old princess, moved down the hall to a smaller, more private, pink and white chamber. Here the old woman sat down on a small sofa near the fireplace, patted the place next to her for Sasha, and nodded her lady-in-waiting and James into a far corner.

"Now, child," said the dowager, "sit by me so we can talk."

"Yes, Aunt Anna," said Sasha.

"Child, don't call me that," said the dowager. "It hurts me so. Don't you think I wish you were my Sasha? I've longed for you so many years I've lost count. Sofya, Sasha's mother and my sister, was dear to me, rest her soul. But my Sasha! It's an awful thing to say of the others, but my Sasha, Sofya's youngest, was my favorite. Such spirit! Such a royal bearing! Such life and joy and courage in her! Ah, she was such a child, such a child!

"I was the one who called her Sasha to begin with, you know. There were two other Tatianas who played at the castle, one the daughter of a countess, the other the daughter of a baron. But Tatiana Alexandrovna was unique. Sasha being the nickname for Alexandra — or Alexandrovna — I simply called her that. Katya, her dear nanny, had such a fit."

Sasha burst into laughter. Without thinking, she reached over to hold the old woman's hand in her own.

"Didn't she!" Sasha agreed. "Katya wanted everyone to call me by my full name. She used to make such a terrible face when you called me across the lawns in summer to go pick flowers. She would always say, 'Why can't Anna Ivanovna call out "Tatiana Alexandrovna" like everyone else?'"

"Stop it, stop that at once!" said the old dowager, growing pale and rising suddenly from the couch. "Those are *my* memories."

"They are mine as well," said Sasha, dropping her head sadly. "But if you don't wish me to share them, to share your life, I will understand. I didn't come here to cause you pain, Aunt Anna. I wanted only to belong somewhere, to have my own family, to come home."

Just as James was about to explode with rage and frustration at the stubborn old woman, the doors to the pink chamber burst open and Prince Stanislaus flew into the room.

"I ought to have a say in this, too, Aunt Anna," said the young prince. "After all, Sasha was to have been my bride, not only heir to the throne. I loved her then, and I love her now. I know perfectly well that she is our Sasha, the friend of my childhood."

"Stanislaus, this is my decision," said the old dowager firmly, though her mouth trembled with sorrow.

Sasha rose from the sofa. James saw how

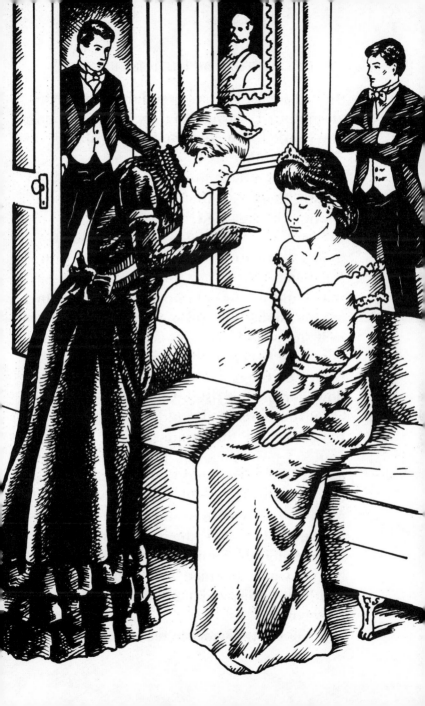

tired she was. He was proud that after a single outburst, Sasha's dignity had returned. She would beg no further, James realized.

"It's all right, Sassu," said Sasha.

No sooner was the word out of Sasha's mouth, than both the old dowager and the young prince gasped.

"You see?" cried the prince triumphantly.

"Oh, my dear, my dear," said Anna Ivanovna.

The old woman plumped down quite unregally on the sofa, pulling Sasha close to her as if she would never let go. Tears streamed down the severe old face. James, watching, could see the resemblance between the old dowager and her sister Ada Ivan.

"No one could have told you your childish pet name for Stanislaus. As a baby, you couldn't pronounce the prince's name. You called him Sassu, and then outgrew it. No one in the world could have taught you that name — only we three and Katya ever knew it. She is, Stanislaus, she is our Sasha!"

James left the family to themselves. It was hard to watch so much joy without emotion, and James preferred to avoid emotion whenever possible.

But out in the wide staircase hall, when he

told Honey the news, she enfolded him in a hug. She knew that sometimes James remembered his days in the orphanage, without parents, without a home. This scene of reunion could not possibly have left him untouched.

James acknowledged Honey's tender insight with the slightest pressure of his arms, a quick look.

"You know, my dear, that there will be a ball tomorow night," James said, changing the subject. "What will you wear?"

"A bathing suit," said Honey, "something in lime green."

She knew perfectly well that James was too distracted to hear. When he was on a case, particularly a delicate one such as this, his mind rarely left it for anything so frivolous as a ball.

What James's mind was on was protecting Sasha until tomorrow's formal acknowledgment and acceptance of her as the heir to the throne of Mornia. Until Sasha was given the scepter bearing the royal Order of the Star, the platinum-and-diamond crown, and the gold-and-ruby ring belonging to the head of state, James planned to stay alert.

"That's nice," he said to Honey absently.

"Let's see if we can find Baron Janos, our friend Laszlo's employer."

The ballroom glittered. Everything was gold and crystal, from the decorated arches and walls to the chandeliers hanging from the vast ceilings, to the musicians' balcony, to the grand staircase. All the nobility of the land would descend that staircase soon, one by one, announced by rank and title by the footmen at the top.

James, Honey, and Sam wandered around the enormous and still-empty ballroom.

"Do you think she's all right?" Honey asked anxiously.

They had not seen Sasha since the evening before, when the old dowager had wept and accepted her as the true princess.

"She's all right," said James. "I only wish we could have found Baron Janos. It makes me nervous, knowing he must still want his own niece on the throne."

"James," said Sam, "you worry too much."

"Sam could be right," said Honey. "Maybe everything's all right."

But Honey had spoken too soon.

The Dowager Princess Anna Ivanovna arrived, Her Royal Highness the Princess Tatiana Alexandrovna on her right, the Prince Stanislaus Petrovich on her left. The three walked regally to the gilt throne chairs on a dais at one end of the grand ballroom. As the music began, all the nobility of Mornia came down the stairs at the other end to be presented to their future ruler. When all had arrived, the old dowager stood, held up her hand to quiet music and people alike, and made the simple presentation of the royal symbols to Sasha.

In just a few moments, the investiture was complete. James and Honey watched as Sasha stood there in the white satin gown and received the scepter with the Order of the Star, the gold-and-ruby ring, then bent her dark head to receive the diamond-and-platinum crown.

"You are sixteen now," the old dowager's voice rang out over the grand ballroom. "You are the heir apparent to the throne of Mornia. When you are eighteen, you shall assume full responsibility as ruler of this realm. Until then, I shall continue to act as your regent, but your regent only. From this moment, you, Tatiana Alexandrovna Ivanova, are Your Royal Highness, Princess of Mornia."

Even Sam's eyes were damp. The crowds of barons and dukes and earls, baronesses and duchesses and countesses, were thrilled. They had a proper court again, with their own lost princess restored to her rightful place.

The orchestra had struck only the first chord to resume its music for dancing, when a small, bent old man, accompanied by a rather dumpy young woman and a swarthy gypsy in a black slouch hat and cape, appeared at the top of the grand staircase.

"Stop!" the old man cried out. "It is my niece who shall rule Mornia, and no other. It is my niece only who has the right, who has been brought up, trained to rule. No impostor shall take her place!"

The dowager princess rose regally, though she looked a little frightened, to protest this sudden outrage.

Sam and James had faded from sight to circle the ballroom unseen. From the top of the grand staircase, they swooped down on Baron Janos and Laszlo.

Sam grabbed the baron, while James took a flying leap and brought Laszlo crashing to the floor.

"Watch it, James, he's got a knife!" Honey yelled, rushing through the crowd to leap on the gypsy assassin and help James.

But it was Her Royal Highness, Princess Tatiana Alexandrovna, who stopped the entire episode as swiftly as if she had fired a shot.

She rose from the central throne to her full regal height. Her voice cut across the entire grand ballroom. As if she had been in fearless and absolute command all her life, she said:

"Stop this at once! How dare you behave like this in my presence?"

Baron Janos's mouth dropped open. Without a second's pause, he shook his dumpy little niece and gave her a push.

"What is the matter with you?" he mumbled. "Go pay your respects to Her Royal Highness."

"It's over," said Sam, standing up and brushing off his evening clothes. "Let's go home."

James and Honey stood also, James completely unruffled as usual, Honey brushing off her evening gown.

"Not quite," said James. "It's not quite over, Sam."

CHAPTER FOURTEEN

Happily Ever After

James had insisted on having a long, lingering waltz with his girl Honey Mack before leaving that grand ballroom. For him, it was not over till then.

"Wasn't it heaven?" Honey sighed, remembering.

The three had flown back home to Nebraska on Sunday, and now were spending their usual Sunday evening in Sam and James's leather-and-brass living room in Kings Rock.

"Did you call Chief Adams?" Sam asked James.

James had just come in from the kitchen with a tray full of cold deviled eggs, a salad, and chocolate eclairs for three. He put the tray on the coffee table in front of the fire Honey had lit, and nodded to Sam.

"I called him. He's already picked up Ratso and his Rat Gang for something else. He'll be delighted, he said, to add kidnapping to the charges. He also wanted to know what we want to do about Ada Ivan — whether we want to press charges of felony child abuse?"

"No point," said Sam. "If she ever gets near another child, I'll have her publicly horsewhipped myself. Anyway, we'd need Sasha to testify, and Sasha's been through too much already. It's enough you saved her, James, knight in shining armor that you are."

James gave a small, warning cough. Sam and Honey had teased him enough, he felt, about his having found the lost princess and returned her to Mornia.

"What about that blasted Laszlo?" said James. "I had enough knives thrown and arrows shot at me to have been dead ten times over."

Sam shook his head. "Out of our jurisdiction," he said. "But Sasha is perfectly capable of dealing with that unholy duo, Baron Janos and his personal assassin."

James didn't look unduly annoyed. Revenge had never interested him. He knew perfectly well that the best revenge was living well and being happy.

"Sasha is happy now. The old dowager is happy now. The prince is happy now. He's got his girl. And I've got mine," said James.

He felt perfectly content, sitting there facing Sam across the fireplace, his arm around his own girl, and his bottle of Perrier beside him.

But the peace did not last long. By the next morning Sam was out of town again, working on a new case. And that afternoon James received an urgent phone call from the Harrington mansion on the Hill.

"It's our son, Dick," said Mr. Harrington. "Something awful has happened. Can you get here right away, James?"

Fifteen minutes later, James was well into *The Mystery of Galaxy Games*.

ABOUT THE AUTHOR

Dale Carlson has been writing stories since she was eight years old. She is the author of more than forty books for young people, including three ALA Notable Books: *The Mountain of Truth, The Human Apes,* and *Girls Are Equal Too.* Her book, *Where's Your Head* won a Christopher Award.

Ms. Carlson lives in New York City.

The James Budd Mysteries